Charles Cameron

A Romance of War

Or how the Cash Goes in Campaigning

Charles Cameron

A Romance of War
Or how the Cash Goes in Campaigning

ISBN/EAN: 9783337067304

Printed in Europe, USA, Canada, Australia, Japan

Cover: Foto ©Andreas Hilbeck / pixelio.de

More available books at **www.hansebooks.com**

A ROMANCE OF WAR;

OR,

HOW THE CASH GOES IN CAMPAIGNING.

COMPILED FROM EVIDENCE GIVEN BEFORE

The Select Committee

On the recent Egyptian Campaign.

BY

CHARLES CAMERON, M.D., LL.D., M.P.

PRICE ONE SHILLING.

LONDON:

BAILLIÈRE, TINDALL, AND COX.

1884.

LONDON :

WITHERBY AND CO., PRINTERS,

325A, HIGH HOLBORN, W.C. ; 74, CORNHILL ; AND
NEWMAN'S COURT, CORNHILL, E.C.

A ROMANCE OF WAR;

OR,

HOW THE CASH GOES IN CAMPAIGNING.

———————

As I have much to say, I shall be very brief in stating my reasons for writing this paper. The Report of the Proceedings of the Select Committee appointed on my motion, in March last, to enquire into the working of the Supply and Transport Services in the Egyptian Campaign has not yet been published, but on the 25th July *The Times* printed a long contribution, "From a Correspondent," professing to sum up the evidence so far as it has gone. The writer's conclusion was that I had failed to make out any case, "that with regard to failures in the working of "the supply and transport services at the seat of war the "evidence seemed to show that there was none," while on the other hand "it seemed manifest that the expedition as a whole "was, from a purely administrative point of view, a success."

From internal evidence it was clear to me that the communication was directly inspired by the War Office. It appeared to me most undesirable in the public interest that, pending not only the report of the Committee but the publication of the evidence taken, this statement should be allowed to pass unchallenged as an impartial summing-up of the case. I therefore wrote to *The Times* traversing its conclusions and promising as soon as Parliament rose to state in detail what some of the principal transport and supply arrangements for the campaign

were, and how they were carried out, so that the public might
judge for themselves as to the boasted " administrative success."
In fulfilment of that promise I now write.

As some failure is admitted in the case of the flour and hay
sent out to Egypt, I will commence with these items.

FLOUR.—Seventy days' supply for the entire force, of
American flour purchased through a firm of London brokers,
was sent out. A large quantity of similar flour shipped during
the China war had gone wrong, and abundant commissariat—not
to speak of Admiralty—experience had shown the impossibility
of relying on flour containing much moisture in hot climates.
American flour was nevertheless selected by the Acting Director of
Supplies and Transport contrary to the advice of the Commissary-
General at head-quarters.   The first cargo was shipped on July
27th, 1882, and on August 31st Sir John Adye telegraphed home
that "it was utterly unfit for use, and was apparently never good."
A reply telegram, sent out on September 1st, stated that the bulk
samples had been that day examined, and were in perfect condition.   It was explained in evidence that the bulk samples were
examined by the brokers.   There was no direct evidence on this
point, however, and the correspondence submitted does not bear
out the assertion, for a letter written by the brokers on September 7th, referring to a paragraph which had appeared in
The Times, makes no allusion to any recent inspection of
bulk samples, but states that the flour was thoroughly examined
before shipment, and was then in good condition.   One thing
was made quite clear, viz., that neither the Director of Supplies
and Transport, the Director of Contracts, nor any official in their
office, ever saw any of the bulk samples.   The flour sent out
was of five different brands, and in the case of one only a sample
of a few ounces was submitted to the purchasing department.
The other four lots were purchased and sent out without any portion of them whatever having been seen by any official of that
department.   Everything—buying, packing and shipping—was

left entirely in the hands of a firm of private brokers paid by a 2½ per cent. commission on their purchases. On the 8th September, a second shipment having in the meanwhile arrived, Sir John Adye wrote home, "The flour from these ships (the "'Osprey' and 'Empusa') is utterly destroyed; the greater "portion of it has arrived in hard, solid blocks, the whole con- "tents of the sack being in many cases an unbroken lump." Other witnesses stated that when the sacks were pulled off, in many cases the flour remained standing like a solid pillar of plaster of Paris. An attempt was made by breaking up and sifting to utilize the flour, but the bread was uneatable, and gave rise to many bitter recriminations recorded in the report of Lord Morley's Committee, and the flour was ultimately sold for making starch. Not till October 10th were sacks of the flour ordered home for analysis, and when in March, 1883, they were submitted for examination to Sir F. Abel, the bulk samples on which the purchases had been made "were not forthcoming," and the minute sample of the first consignment which had been lying about in the War Office, was in such a state that that chemist refused to examine it.

That flour, properly selected and properly packed, can with-stand the Egyptian climate was shown by the fact that Australian and Navy flour sent out in September remained perfectly good in February.

HAY.—Among the compressed hay purchased for the expedition was 2372 tons, bought at a cost of £20,592 from Mr. Cussans, an army contractor in Liverpool. The hay was purchased by that gentleman from upwards of 100 sources, so that its quality naturally varied, but it was bought as "best upland meadow hay," 1099 tons of this hay was sent out for the use of English horses. The Commissary-General of the expedition stated that he never saw a truss of this brand that was not more or less damaged. His successor in Egypt said that hundreds of the bales were filled with outside wrappers of hay, and that he saw issued bales containing pieces of brick, stones, rubbish, and refuse straw rolled up into hard lumps. The landing officer at Ismailia stated that he opened about 100 bales of the same hay per the "Osmanli," and found in many of them lumps of whitish clay and roots weighing as much as a pound and a half, and that "in some of the trusses the hay "appeared to be made of old twisted ropes from the other "trusses." Captain Lea stated, "it was the worst quality he "ever saw in his life." He thought it must have been grown on low, marshy soil and flooded, as it contained sand and clay. The principal veterinary surgeon described it as of "the most infa- "mous quality," and composed in large part of "the wiry, pliable "sort of hay used at home for packing china in hampers." And so on. There was a consensus of evidence that it was not best upland meadow hay, but contained rushes and lowland grasses. Another 526 tons of this hay were sent out to Egypt for the use of the Indian contingent. Complaints were received of its quality, and when 150 tons of it which remained on hand at the termination of operations was examined, with a view to being taken over by the British Government, it was refused as being "water meadow hay of a very inferior description." A third por- tion of this hay was supplied for use in transports, and there were complaints about it too. Another 556 tons, stored in Liverpool, was on November 29th condemned by a Special Board as "of "inferior quality, of lowland and water meadow growth, and "deficient in feeding properties for troop-horses." This batch was sold for £2 11s. 6d. per ton, realising a loss of £3058, besides cost of storage. In consequence of the capture of Cairo, Mr. Cussans's last contract was cancelled and he received com- pensation to the extent of £1564. In adjusting this compen- sation the Director of Contracts, according to his own statement, "complimented Mr. Cussans on the way in which he had done "his work, and said that they were all exceedingly obliged to "him for the manner in which he had met the service." Mr. Cussans told us that he had no reason to believe that his hay had caused any dissatisfaction until he read in the newspapers the statements made regarding it by witnesses before our committee. So far as he was concerned he seems to have had no reason to complain, for he confessed to a profit of about 30s. a ton (or £3500 on the contract), besides his £1500 of compensation; he had been complimented by the Director of Contracts, and up to the end of June last he enjoyed army contracts averaging £1200 per month.

SUPPLIES.—On behalf of the Office of Supplies and Transport, it was urged that 50 separate stores were shipped by that department, and only two proved bad. As a fact, 45 of the 50 were supplied by the Admiralty, bought on the faith of some particular trade mark or brand, or on approval by the Medical Department. Flour, hay, potatoes, oats and cheese, alone were purchased in the open market on the sole responsibility of the Supply Department. The flour and hay I have disposed of. The potatoes were apparently all right, but their total value was only £174. There is a dispute about the quality of the oats, and no samples were forthcoming to decide the question, and the cheese, though good, did not reach the troops till after they were in Cairo.

THE IRON RATION.—One topic constantly coming before the Committee was the Iron Ration. This, Colonel Tulloch explained, was the name given by the Germans to the celebrated *erbswurst*, or pea-soup sausage ration, which each German soldier is compelled to carry, which he is only permitted to consume on an emergency and by order of a superior officer, and which if he makes away with without permission he is liable to be shot. Tinned *erbswurst* and tinned tongues were sent out to Egypt as an iron ration. They did not arrive till September 8th, then they were carried on to Suez, and they were not available for issue till we got to Cairo. Finally, of 9300 lbs. of *erbswurst* sent out only 4445 lbs. arrived fit for use, the other 4855 lbs., owing to faulty packing, being so damaged in transit that they had to be condemned.

THE MEAT CONTRACT.—Of the contracts submitted to the Committee one of the clearest and most business-like was for the supply of fresh meat to the Army. It was for a minimum amount of 140,000 lbs. of meat per week, and was terminable at any time after the 29th November, 1882, on a month's notice. About the 19th September the General in Egypt, apparently under a misapprehension on this point, ordered further supplies to be stopped. On being informed of this, the Acting Surveyor-General of Ordnance, by whose department the contract had been made, instead of telegraphing back that the contract was binding until November 29th, according to the Director of Contracts "thought that he could do nothing but support the decision of the General on the spot." The contractor was written to and lawyers called in, and finally the contract was allowed to run on considerably beyond the date at which it was terminable, but the result of the interruption was a large claim on the part of the contractor, which was not settled when the Committee rose. The meat delivered under the contract is described as good, though dear.

A PHANTOM PIER.—In organizing the campaign the main reliance for transport on the line of communication had been placed on the railway. Arabi might destroy the road, but it would be easy to repair it, and rails, engines, and plant were among the equipment sent out. It was known that the facilities for landing at Ismailia were wretched, and a wooden pier designed to be erected on sunk barges was constructed at Woolwich. It carried rails for through connection with the railway, and was furnished with steam cranes and a big shear for lifting heavy weights. Colonel Salmond, R.E., was ordered to inspect it at Woolwich, and then to proceed to Ismailia to erect it. He arrived at Ismailia per the "Viking," on August 21st, the day after the first troops landed, but the pier and appliances were sent out by three other vessels, the last two of which reached that port 15 and 18 days later respectively. By that time it was too late. Other arrangements had been made; the pier was not erected, the cranes were not unloaded, and as for the big shear one of its legs had been left behind.

RAILWAY CORPS OF ROYAL ENGINEERS.—To repair and utilize the railway a Railway Corps of Engineers had been organized in England. It was commanded by Colonel Wallace, R.E., an officer of large railway experience. Some of the other officers and men composing it seem to have possessed special knowledge of different departments of railway work, but the majority knew practically nothing beyond what they were able to pick up in the course of a ten days' run on the London, Chatham and Dover, and South-Eastern Railways. Colonel Wallace asked for 200 officers and men, but so many not being available, he only got 100. He asked to have them supplemented by a corps of skilled civilians, but this was refused. Colonel Wallace arrived at Ismailia with the first troops. The most pressing work was the construction of a railway of 1000 yards between the railway station and the central landing jetty. Five miles of rails had been sent out from England, but as they did not arrive for several days afterwards, Colonel Wallace had to seize a lot of light and faulty rails, which he found lying in a depôt of the Canal Company. The Railway Corps did not land till the 24th, so he was obliged to wait many hours before he could get a fatigue party. The rails being laid down, Colonel Wallace was ordered off to Suez, and Colonel Salmond took up the work for two days, when the Railway Corps at length appeared. Meanwhile the aid of a civilian contractor had been called in, and the railway was completed on the 27th. This 1000 yards of railway, completed with the aid of a civilian contractor and civilian labour, took five days to construct, or at the rate of 200 yards a day. The

Railway Company of Engineers did not land till three days after it had been commenced, and it was still later before the rails which they brought with them were available. Finally, owing to defective material and construction, the railway was so badly laid that not even the lightest engine could ever run upon it, and all the traffic had to be worked by horses and mules.

THE TELEGRAPH CORPS.—"With a single line," said Sir John Adye, "it is almost impossible to work without a "telegraph." In order to be prepared for emergencies Great Britain has for many years past kept up a special telegraph corps of Royal Engineers. A company of this corps was despatched to Egypt, but did not arrive till August 28th. Meanwhile the engagements of El Magfar and Mashamah had been fought, and on the day of the arrival of the corps at Ismailia our troops at Kassassin sustained the most serious attack made upon them during the war. Pending the arrival of the telegraph corps, Colonel Salmond had got together a few men from the Engineers who understood something about telegraphy, and he had discovered an Arab platelayer who he thought knew how to solder wires and "make earth." "I took hold of a piece of "copper and a piece of wire," said Colonel Salmond in his evidence, "and pointed to the ground. He understood what was "meant. I made him make a joint then and there, and I saw "that he understood what I meant." The Arab was sent forward, and he repaired the wires which the Egyptians had cut. Perfection could hardly be expected of a service so roughly improvised, and the Principal Medical Officer complained that when he sent down batches of sick and telegraphed their despatch they frequently arrived before the telegrams, greatly to the disturbance of his arrangements.

LOCOMOTIVE ENGINES.—Four small engines were purchased, in England, for the use of the expedition. They did not, however, arrive till a fortnight after the troops landed at Ismailia. Others were purchased and requisitioned at Alexandria, and went to Ismailia with the troops. The Admiralty vessel "Recovery," fitted with a crane to lift heavy weights, had been arranged for to assist in landing these engines and other weighty material, but she did not arrive for 11 days afterwards. By what Colonel Wallace described as "a piece of great luck," the line from Nefiche to Suez had been left open, and the engines were sent on there. At Suez an antiquated floating derrick, worked by belting instead of gearing, was secured. The small engines were got out easily enough, but with the full-sized ones it was dangerous work. The naval officer who conducted the operation described it thus:—"Those two last engines were a heavy lift, and we had " to screw the safety-valve of the crane's boiler before we could " stir them. The Arab stoker bolted when he saw the steam " pressure go above 40 lbs., but we got it up to 52 with a trusty " English stoker, and out came the engines, * * * * I " think the man who sits on a safety-valve, and knows his own " danger, deserves the Victoria Cross." With the third big engine the crane broke down.

REGIMENTAL TRANSPORT.—Each regiment on active service is supposed to constitute a complete unit, and embraces its own transport. The Egyptian is said to have been the first campaign in which the regiments embarked with their regimental transport generally complete. On the advance to El Magfar, eight miles from Ismailia, on August 24th, regimental transport was the only transport relied on, for none of the Department transport had disembarked, except a few horses and mules intended for the medical services, but actually employed in dragging trucks on the railway. None of the auxiliary transport had arrived, and the canal (on which there were only a few native fruit boats employed in supplying a detachment of troops at Nefiche) had been ordered to be kept shut for fear of wasting the precious water. Following the troops, Colonel Harrison,

Senior Staff Officer on the Line of Communication, found that the regimental transport which was to have carried the supplies, "could not get along through the sand, and that "provisions and stores of all sorts were scattered along the road "to lighten men and horses." "It was evident that if the "troops were to maintain their position supplies must be sent "up at once." The railway had been cut in two places, but Colonel Harrison discovered that the Egyptians had dammed the canal at El Magfar, and thus afforded an unexpected deliverance from the difficulty. After consultation with Lord Wolseley Colonel Harrison galloped back to Ismailia, and, after considerable parley, got the Admiral to open the canal and place boats on it, and so sent on provisions. This is an example of the breakdown of the regimental transport at a most critical juncture. The General's order was that three and a half days' food should be carried with the advance, and Colonel Harrison stated that on the faith of that order his department "did not expect to have to send them anything for three days at least." According to Deputy Assistant Commissary-General Baker two days' provisions were placed in the regimental transport carts, but when on the morning of the 25th the troops halted at Mahuta, ten miles distant from Ismailia, the transport did not come up till next day, and some was two days before it rejoined the regiments. "The same thing," he added, "more "or less happened on every occasion when reserve rations had to "be carried by the regimental transport."

THE DEPARTMENTAL TRANSPORT.—The Departmental or Divisional Transport required to make each division a unit should have marched along with it.

The first division landed on August 21st and 22nd. It was not joined by any of its divisional transport till the 28th. The cavalry division landed on August 22nd, and was not joined by any of its divisional transport till September 4th. The second division, which did not leave Ismailia till well on in September, was the only division which marched with its divisional transport.

The establishment of drivers and horses employed in the departmental transport, kept as low as possible in time of peace, is augmented in time of war. The men supplied for the purpose, in the case of the Egyptian campaign, were to a large extent drawn from the infantry reserve, and militia recruits, and knew nothing of riding or of horses. Captain Lea, describing the march of his company from Woolwich to the Albert Docks, stated that several of the men had to be put upon the horses before they left with them, and several fell off on the march, but happily they had no serious accident. The heavy waggons sent out from England were useless, except in towns.

Auxiliary Transport.—This was intended to consist of 3600 pack mules, 1500 drivers, and 150 headmen. In order to ensure that this number should be available arrangements were made for the purchase of 3800 mules, and 800 more belonging to Government in Natal were ordered to Egypt. Besides these, 1000 extra were ordered later to make good casualties. Altogether 5109 mules were bought at a cost of £131,290, exclusive, except in one instance, of freight, and 657 more were shipped at Natal. Of these 5766 animals only 2225 landed in Egypt before Tel-el-Kebir, but of that 2225, 758, part of two lots purchased at Beyrout and Smyrna, were unfit for work, and 246 were required to complete regimental and divisional transport. Instead, therefore, of the 3600 animals intended for auxiliary transport, only 1221 were ever available for the purpose. Of these the first lot (about 300) did not arrive at Ismailia till nine days after the troops had landed.

Intention and Realization.—Up to the time when the railway to the jetty was complete, and the first engine ran, a period during which the whole traffic had to be worked by horses and mules, only 255 horses and 123 mules, or 378 animals instead of 4700, the establishment laid down for departmental and auxiliary transport, had landed. Three days later, at the date of the first through train to Kassassin, only 584 animals had landed. All these animals belonged to the departmental transport. Evidence was given that the 3600 auxiliary transport animals were estimated for, not for the purpose of forwarding supplies along the line of communication, but for distribution from the different depôts, and as the first batch of 150 of these animals only left Ismailia on September 3rd, a fortnight after the troops had landed, the public may judge how far the coincidence of realization and intention justified the boast of an " administrative success."

GOVERNMENT MULES AT NATAL.—The British Government had between 1300 and 1400 mules on hand at Natal, and were selling them off to reduce the Natal establishment to its peace footing of 500. On July 5th, orders were telegraphed to stop sales, with the view of utilizing the animals in Egypt. Evidence was given that steamers for their transport could easily have been chartered and fitted out at Durban, and that that would have been the usual course. Instead of applying to their naval agent at Natal, the Admiralty, through a broker, entered into negotiations with the "Notting Hill," a vessel lying at Algoa Bay laden with wool, wasted several days waiting for her to arrange to get rid of her cargo, then chartered her at the rate of £4021 per month, paid her £3000 besides for expenses of getting rid of cargo, and allowed her a week, or close on another £1000, to discharge cargo and proceed to the Admiralty establishment at Simon's Bay to refit. There she was refitted for mules, the mangers being in many cases fixed up where the mules' tails were to be. So much time was lost that instead of taking in forage purchased for the purpose at Durban, where it would have had to be embarked in lighters, she went to Cape Town for a fresh lot. Small-pox was raging there, and when she got to Durban she was put into quarantine and further delay incurred. Finally she loaded her mules, and on September 5th sailed for Egypt. Small-pox broke out on the voyage, and she arrived at Aden, five days from Suez, on September 21st, or eight days after Tel-el-Kebir. At Aden she was intercepted and sent on to Bombay, where her mules were sold to the Indian Government at prices ranging from £25 to £27 10s. per head. That Government seem to have driven anything but a hard bargain, as the Secretary of State for War had authorized the sale of the animals to them at £15 per head. But even the £17,000 or £18,000 paid by the Indian Treasury left John Bull but little to congratulate himself on, for he had to pay £13,159 for hire of the "Notting Hill," besides cost of fitting out, forage, and I know not how many thousand pounds for pay and maintenance to Bombay and back of 212 drivers and 16 conductors hired for six months at wages ranging from 4s. 6d. to 12s. 6d. per day.

THE BEYROUT AND SMYRNA MULES.—When it was resolved to purchase mules in Ottoman territory on the Levant, the Commissary-General at head-quarters, accompanied by the Director of Supplies and Transport, waited upon the Surveyor-General of Ordnance (Sir John Adye) to object on account, amongst other reasons, of the danger of interference by the Turkish Government. The objection was, however, overruled, and on July 22nd the order was given to purchase. Seven hundred mules were bought at Smyrna and 800 at Beyrout, at a cost of £36,950, including freight of the Smyrna lot to Port Said. Of the Beyrout lot we have little information. They were bought on a contract made with a Mr. Christian by the General Officer in Cyprus. The Porte laid an embargo on their exportation, which was removed on September 4th. On September 9th, 498 of them were disembarked at Ismailia from the "Assyrian Monarch," and on the 11th, a board appointed to inspect them pronounced 344 unfit for immediate use. The rest were disembarked on the 13th and 15th, by which time Tel-el-Kebir had fallen.

A Chapter of Accidents.—Major Carré was the officer sent out to purchase the Smyrna mules, and a full history of his misadventures is contained in a letter from himself, which was laid before the Committee. He purchased a number of animals which the veterinary sent out to advise him advised him to reject. He accepted the offer of a room in the contractor's country house, and left the branding irons in the charge of the contractor's men. After considerable trouble from the Turkish authorities, on August 23rd the embargo on the exportation of the mules was removed. The embargo on the shipment of muleteers continued, but Major Carré, under the circumstances, " considered himself justified in disregarding a published order " of the Sultan's, and secretly engaged men at Smyrna, who " were Turkish subjects, to accompany the mules, and placed " them on board the hired ships 'Pelayo' and 'Camerata.' " These vessels lay within a mile and a half of the pier, and were consequently in Turkish waters. The mules were embarked in lighters by the contractor. On the 28th, when the shipment commenced, " certain sums of money were paid to the Turkish " authorities to allow the embarkation to proceed without " molestation." On the following day there was some dispute, and a company of soldiers in charge of an officer, who said he was acting under orders, came upon the scene and arrested some muleteers who were in the lighters. The officer wished to search the vessels for Turkish subjects. This Major Carré refused to allow, and, after some difficulty, persuaded him to return with his prisoners to the Governor, whereupon, leaving 89 mules in the hands of the contractor, Major Carré at once ordered the captains of the vessels to sail. Forage for the mules had been previously embarked, but all the bran had been placed on board one vessel and all the barley on the other. The natives embarked turned out mutinous, and it was with difficulty the mules were watered and fed. Arrived at Port Said, the captains of the vessels refused without a large extra payment to go on to Ismailia, and the mules were transhipped on board the "Viking." The muleteers continued mutinous, refused to work, and attempted to escape by swimming ashore, and a certain number of them got away. A naval guard was put on board, and boats cruised round the ship by night and day. On the 6th and 7th September the mules were disembarked at Ismailia. A lot of them were thrown into the water to swim ashore, and the number received was thirteen short of that tallied on board the "Viking" at Port Said. Of the 602 landed the principal veterinary surgeon reported only 186 fit for duty, and on September 11th (two days before Tel-el-Kebir) a board of officers pronounced 414 unfit for immediate work. Sore backs, wounds, catarrh and old age (18 to 25 years) are mentioned as the principal causes of unfitness. As the mules stood in the depôt at Smyrna Major Carré declares them to have been "as good a lot of transport mules as he had ever seen." He can only account for the state in which they were landed at Ismailia by the fact that they "were either suffering from the " journey or else that the Turkish and Greek servants who " brought the mules from the depôt to the pier surreptitiously " changed the good ones for those rejected. He cannot state " that this was done, but his suspicions were raised when he heard " some time after the Committee had assembled at Ismailia " that mules had been found without brands on the feet, whilst " every mule he passed was branded."

The opinion of Colonel Owen Lanyon, Commandant at the Base, on the Beyrout and Smyrna consignments, is contained in a minute dated September 12th, 1882, which was laid before the Committee.—"It seems to me a very " serious matter," he wrote, "that out of 1100 mules " purchased for immediate use there should be 758 unfit for " work when landed * * * We cannot sell them here, and " they would not be worth the expense of sending to another " market. Meanwhile they are a great expense and trouble to " the Government."

C

As will be observed, this was written two days before the fall of Cairo brought the war to the close.

MULES IN BRITISH TERRITORY.— Assistant Commissary-General Elmes, who had charge of the Government depôt of mules at Natal before referred to, stated that besides 876 mules above the number required to keep up his establishment, in hand when the order was given to stop sales, he could easily have bought 1000 more in that colony, and that there was always plenty of steam transport available at or near Durban, and facilities on the spot for fitting it up.

On July 26th enquiries were made at the request of Lord Wolseley as to whether the Indian Government could despatch to Egypt 1500 efficient mules or ponies, fully equipped, with drivers and officers. On July 29th a reply was received from the Viceroy that 1000 mules, with equipment and establishment, could be got off after the Indian contingent. That contingent arrived at Suez on August 22nd, but on August 10th a telegram had been sent out stating that the mules were not wanted.

DRIVERS.—It was intended that 1500 drivers and 150 headmen, interpreters, and artificers should be provided for the auxiliary transport. As a matter of fact, only 576 were brought to Egypt. It was in the first place intended to have got drivers from the Punjaub, but in consequence of the obvious importance of obtaining men to whose language the mules were accustomed, that idea was given up, and it was resolved to hire drivers in the countries in which the animals were purchased. Of the 576 drivers who arrived, some 200 were hired in Cyprus. Orders had been given that they were not to be paid more than 2s. per day, a sum which offered no inducement to natives to engage. This difficulty, however, the officer who hired them got over by promising 3s. from the date of embarkation. At first they were not allowed rations, but as it was found that without rations they could not be kept from deserting, a bread ration was finally sanctioned. The officer who hired them understood that he was authorized to promise them clothing, and they were engaged on this footing. It turned out that clothing, though specially asked for by the Commissary-General, had been disallowed by the Surveyor-General of Ordnance (Sir John Adye), who, however, sanctioned the issue of badges showing that the men belonged to our army. The badges never arrived. In Egypt all other attempts to obtain the promised clothing having failed, the men rebelled, and sitting down refused to march through the burning sand unless boots were supplied to them. This argument prevailed, and boots were issued.

When the Cyprus drivers landed at Ismailia there was a great demand for labour. Some commissariat officers were giving labourers as much as 6s. and 7s. a day, and the drivers having nothing to distinguish them occasioned a great deal of trouble by deserting to the more lucrative employment. Finally, a civilian contractor, offering still higher wages—8s. or 10s. a day—they deserted to him, and there was further trouble in identifying and recovering them.

Major Carré, who bought the mules in Smyrna, contracted with Messrs. Gilchrist, Walker, and Co., of Constantinople, for the hire of 366 Montenegrin muleteers and headmen. The Turkish Government forbade their embarkation, and imprisoned them. We paid them an indemnity of £835, and there the transaction ended.

Drivers were hired in Malta. Notwithstanding the decision of the Surveyor-General not to allow uniform, they were provided with clothing and sandals by direction of the military authorities at home, and the only objection stated with regard to them was that they knew nothing about mules.

DRIVERS FROM BRITISH DEPENDENCIES.—A batch of 212 men was sent from Natal with the mules shipped from that colony, but arrived late, went on to Bombay, and were sent back. They were hired locally, and received a six months' engagement at 4s. 6d. to 5s. per day besides clothing.

As I have said, it was originally intended to hire drivers in India, but that idea, for reasons before stated, was abandoned. Subsequently the original intention was reverted to, and on August 10th orders were sent out for the hire of 500 drivers for service with the British Auxiliary Transport. They were organized and sent off, but arrived after the war was over. Their pay was a little over 10 rupees a month.

USELESS PACK SADDLES.—It had been arranged that the pack saddles carried by the mules purchased for the auxiliary transport should be bought along with them, so that each mule should land with its equipment fitted and complete. This arrangement was departed from, but between 1500 and 1600 Turkish and Syrian pack saddles purchased at £1 a-piece were landed at Ismailia. The mode of fastening on the loads being somewhat complicated they required skilled muleteers to load them, and these being wanting the saddles were useless. Some were carried from the ships and piled in heaps in the camp, but were never used, and others were unloaded and sent direct into store. Luckily, English pack saddles enough for the mules received had been sent out from home.

CAMELS.—In the earlier arrangements for the campaign, it was proposed to purchase camels for transport purposes at Cyprus and Beyrout. Various witnesses gave evidence, that camels would have been much preferable to mules in a country like Egypt. Enormous numbers of camels were procured in India for the Afghan War, and there are considerable numbers of them in Cyprus, but these places were not resorted to. On July 27, Admiral Hoskins was instructed to take steps for hiring what camel transport could be hired in the neighbourhood of the Suez Canal. He at once reported that till the troops arrived, the Bedouins were afraid to take service. Professor

Palmer and Captain Gill were also sent on that mission to purchase camels from the Bedouins in which they lost their lives, and on September 1st, Lord Wolseley telegraphed home from Ismailia as follows :—" An army operating from this base could " only be fed by a railway, a canal, or a host of camels, owing " to the absence of roads and the great depth of sand. The " obstruction to canal and railway caused by the enemy was " considerable. Camels can only be obtained from Bedouins, " the assistance of some of whom I hope to secure shortly."

Meanwhile, on August 24th, Colonel Tulloch, of the Intelligence Department, submitted an offer of 300 camels from a Bedouin at Kantara, forty miles up the canal, and pointed out that there were 200 Egyptian prisoners at Port Said, who were all fellaheen, and quite understood camel driving. The offer was refused, as Sir John Adye had decided that camels might be hired, so that the services of their owners as drivers might be secured, but must not be purchased. Colonel Tulloch, who employed Egyptian prisoners as drivers for some camels which he bought, found them faithful and trustworthy, dreading dismissal to Arabi more than anything else. On August 25th another offer of 1000 camels, at £16 a head, was received from Syria through Colonel Tulloch, but it, too, was refused for the same reason. The first consignment of mules for auxiliary transport was not landed for about a week afterwards.

LABOURERS.—Before starting for Egypt, the Commissary-General with the expedition asked for 400 labourers to assist in unloading ships and other work in Egypt. The Surveyor-General " did not altogether decline, but said that he would " rather wait till they got out, till it was seen what would be " required." Nevertheless, on July 26th, the Adjutant-General telegraphed to Malta asking whether 300 labourers could be hired there, and a reply was received that a limited number might be engaged at 3s. a day, and recommending advertisement. Apparently nothing further was done. Subsequently enquiries were made as to the possibility of hiring labourers at Trieste. On August 12th the General at Alexandria telegraphed asking result of action about labourers, and on the 14th he was advised by wire that labourers were not procurable at Malta, and that no reply had been received from Trieste.

LABOUR AT ISMAILIA.—Various officers gave evidence as to the great scarcity of labour. The majority spoke in favour of civilian labour, objecting to military, on the ground that fatigue parties are difficult to procure and not being paid dislike the duty, and that they are changed so frequently that they have no time to become acquainted with the work required of them. As a matter of fact, labourers on the spot commanded their own terms. Colonel Wallace, Director of Railways, described his experience rather amusingly. He had "gangs of " all sorts of scoundrels doing platelaying and that sort of " work." Some of them he had brought from Alexandria, and " others came in from day to day to Ismailia to take service under " three or four different officers, and try to put in an appearance " at pay time with each of them." " He used to consider himself " lucky when he could get them at 6s. per day, then the price " went up to 10s., and he was told that the Commissariat men " and his fellows had all disappeared except one gang. He " managed to keep some thirty or forty of these men, and they " used to come to him periodically for an increase of pay, " saying that the other departments were paying so much they " could not stop." Colonel Wallace had to pay as much as 8s. a-day. Ultimately, after Cairo had been occupied, on September 16th 320 Somali labourers arrived from Aden.

FARRIERS.—Although the establishment of regimental transport for each regiment included 49 animals, and the auxiliary transport was to have consisted of 3600 animals, no provision was made for shoeing them. An order had been given that a certain number of artificers in each infantry regiment should be instructed in shoeing, but it appeared that this was a dead letter. Before starting for Egypt the Principal Veterinary Surgeon of the expedition was given to understand that a force of farriers would be sent out for the animals of the auxiliary transport, but they never arrived, and the departmental transport, having only its peace establishment of farriers, could do nothing to assist.

FORGE CARTS.—In former wars, according to the Principal Veterinary Surgeon of the expedition, it was customary for coal and iron to be supplied to the farriers, who were required to make horseshoes in the field. For this purpose they were supplied with heavy forge carts which it required six horses to draw along good roads. In Egypt, instead of adopting this system, ready-made horseshoes were supplied. But the forge carts were sent out nevertheless. In Egypt twelve horses had to be harnessed to them; but even that number could not get them along, and finally they were sent up by railway. Light, portable forges carried on a mule's back, according to the Principal Veterinary Surgeon, would have answered every purpose, but none were available.

MEDICAL TRANSPORT.—When the war was being arranged for, a number of mules which had been trained to carry *cacolets* or litters for the ambulance service, were taken to assist in making up regimental transport. They were replaced by untrained animals from the north of Spain. The ambulance animals thus recruited, and consisting of 79 horses and 123 mules, landed at Ismailia two days before any others and were at once appropriated for the all-important work of dragging trucks on the railway. In anticipation of the battle of El Magfar on August 25th, Sir James Hanbury, the principal medical officer, applied for other mules and got 15. They were untrained animals, and before applying them to the purpose of carrying the wounded, Sir James ordered a transport driver to mount one of them. "He shot him

" over his head like a catapult." Sir James did not allow any of the wounded to be placed upon those mules. Even stretchers were not available on that occasion, for the eight stretchers per regiment allowed were carried by the regimental transport, stuck far behind in the sand.

The country paid £59,717 for hire and other charges of the hospital and transport ship, "Carthage," besides expenses of fitting her out as a hospital. Her pay commenced on July 25th, and was at the rate of over £7500 per month, or about £250 per day. She was fitted out for 82 sick, 146 convalescents, and 20 officers in cabins. It did not transpire how long it took to fit her out, but she arrived at Malta on August 17th, and remained there twenty-six hours coaling. She then proceeded to Alexandria, arriving after the expedition had sailed, and remained there forty hours, and did not arrive at Ismailia till the 25th. She had three field hospitals on board, but she was not unloaded till the 27th or 28th, as Sir James Hanbury explained, "because there was no "transport." I need not recapitulate Sir James Hanbury's tale. It may be summed up in two sentences—inability to move forward field hospitals for want of transport, and army hospital corps taken away from their proper duties to remedy as far as they could the want of transport and labour.

ROUNDABOUT ROUTES.—The Household Cavalry, stationed in London, embarked for Egypt at the Albert Docks, directly opposite Woolwich, from which place they drew their equipment. The easiest mode of delivering it would have been to send it across the river and place it on board the vessels in which they were to go out. At first they were informed that this would be done, but at the last moment they received notice that their equipment would be handed to them in London. It was accordingly sent up to London from Woolwich, and they had to cart it back again on the other side of the river to the Albert Docks. Captain Knocker, Deputy Assistant Commissary-General, detailed a very similar experience. The "Dacca," which took out part of his Commissariat Company, sailed from the Albert Docks. Their stores and equipments were drawn from Woolwich. Instead, however, of these being sent across the river and embarked at the Albert Docks, they were sent down to Portsmouth and there put on board the "Dacca."

CANDLES FOR OIL LAMPS.—In the departmental report of Commissary-General Sir Edward Morris, drawn up at the end of the war, there occurred this paragraph :—

"Candles are very preferable to oil for general purposes of "lighting, but the equipment of lamps and lanterns should be "allowed to suit. If you issue to a man an oil lamp he "naturally expects to receive the oil."

Asked as to the meaning of this paragraph, Sir Edward stated that one department had sent out the candles and another the oil lamps. The following day the Assistant-Director of Supplies brought up a lantern and showed how, by taking out the mechanism which supported the wick, a candle could be fitted into it. Sir Edward Morris replied that the lamp produced was a distinguishing lantern, used as a sign at the tents of general officers, and that he referred to the globular brass lamps issued to the troops. On a later day a storekeeper from Woolwich was brought up to exhibit the lamp referred to, and demonstrate the frivolous nature of the objection. He showed how by cutting a piece out of one side of the bottom of a candle and removing the holder of the wick of the lamp, the candle could be fixed in the oil reservoir. The defence appeared to be complete, when one of the members of the Committee suggested that the candle should be lighted and the lamp put together. It was then found that the flame and all but a couple of inches of the candle were swallowed up in the brass chimney with which the glass globe of the lamp was surmounted. The candle, emitting a dense smoke, burned within the chimney about two hours before any of its flame was visible, and by the time the light became fully disclosed only about an inch of candle remained. These lamps were intended for the use of men engaged in outdoor work at night.

BRANDING IRONS.—It was intended to establish a mule depôt at Cyprus, and the Commissary-General, before the departure of the officer who was to take charge of the depôt, sent in a demand for branding irons to the Ordnance Department, informing them that a certain officer at Woolwich could show them exactly what was wanted. That officer was not referred to, and, no branding irons being forthcoming, the officer sent to Cyprus got them made by his farrier. The correspondence on the subject was not, however, lost sight of, and this year, while the Committee was sitting, patterns of branding irons were submitted by the Ordnance Department to the Commissariat for approval. They were produced before the Committee. An iron to brand a figure or a broad arrow should, of course, be open at the back, so that only the outline of the number or design intended to be marked on the animal may be burnt. The patterns which after nearly two years' consideration had been submitted by the Ordnance Department, had the broad arrow and numbers slightly raised upon solid backs, so that when heated they would have produced on any animal to which they were applied a huge burn, in which no trace of the figure or broad arrow would be visible.

A TELL-TALE TELEGRAM.—A quantity of hay purchased in the West of England for the expedition was sent to Woolwich to be pressed. On July 27th Mr. Blunt, Senior Commissariat Officer at Woolwich, telegraphed as follows:—
" None of the West of England hay come in is good enough for
" pressing. Our hydraulic press must stop to-morrow for want of
" hay. I have therefore purchased forty tons from Underwood at
" £8 10s., bands excluded. Underwood will give £5 for the thirty
" tons of West hay as it stands." This telegram was addressed to the

Director of Supplies and Transport, and by him passed on to the Director of Contracts for remarks. The Director of Contracts wrote on the back as follows:—" One of the objects of " buying and having the inspection in the Western District " was that the excessive rigour of the Woolwich inspection " might be avoided. I do not think the A.C.G." (that is, Mr. Blunt) " would pass any of the hay that has been pressed " elsewhere. Will you make it clear that he is to press the hay " as it comes ? " The telegram with this endorsation was apparently laid on a table on which the Director of Supplies and Transport was drafting answers to letters submitted to him, and a clerk, taking it up with the correspondence, mistook the remarks on the back of the telegram for an answer. Procuring a telegraph form, therefore, he copied the remarks and wired them as a message from the Director of Supplies and Transport to Mr. Blunt. That gentleman, naturally rather surprised on its receipt, telegraphed back that he could not undertake the responsibility of passing the hay, and did not quite understand the message. Attention being thus called to the mistake, a reply was sent, ordering the telegram to be cancelled.

A quantity of the West of England hay having been condemned, I got the Committee to order the correspondence relating to the subject. It was produced, but without the telegrams I have quoted, and of the existence of which I was aware. Their suppression was explained on the ground that they were properly departmental minutes; but however applicable that term might be to one of the telegrams, it was certainly not applicable to either of those in which the Commissariat Officer at Woolwich expressed his opinion of the hay sent in. A Board held on the hay pronounced it " not best upland meadow hay of " last year's growth, and not in the primest condition ; " and stated their opinion " that the purchaser had either purchased " inferior hay, or he had not taken the necessary steps to ensure " the safe delivery of the purchase."

FINANCIAL CONTROL AND AUDIT.—This hay was condemned and re-sold, and the public bore the loss. That loss was only a trifle, apparently between £100 and £200, besides freight to Woolwich ; but it is noteworthy that, owing to the technical fact that the hay had never been "received into charge," it was the sole case that came before the Committee in which the Exchequer and Audit Department asked for an explanation of any loss incurred through the condemnation of stores after purchase. Even in this case the explanation given was partial, as it omitted the proportionately heavy loss on railway freight.

This seems to have been the solitary instance in connection with the Campaign in which anybody was called to account for anything.

REVIEW.—I have not attempted to exhaust the evidence laid before the Select Committee as to the chaotic state in which the Egyptian Campaign found our system of supply and transport. I have said nothing about the conflicting evidence as to responsibility, or blame bandied about from official to official, and department to department. I have said nothing about the absolute want of organization of the auxiliary transport, the looseness of some of the contracts, nor the system of transport by sea, for which the country paid over £860,000 for hire of vessels, besides a large sum extra for freights. I have said nothing about the difficulties experienced by myself in extracting certain items of information, and the apparent impossibility of getting others which with an efficient system of accounts would have been readily forthcoming. I have suggested no plan of reform. The Committee, in reporting the evidence to the House, has asked for re-appointment. It will be for them to deal with these matters, and, if they think proper, to apportion praise or blame to individuals and departments. I have contented myself with putting into connected shape certain easily intelligible facts which have been laid before Parliament in the evidence taken.

THE ANSWER TO MY CASE.—The answer to my case has been made in evidence given by Sir John Adye, who was first the Surveyor-General of Ordnance ministerially responsible for all the arrangements at home, and afterwards Chief of the Staff in Egypt. It has been repeated in the official communication to *The Times*, to which I have before referred. That answer consists in the general assertion that no transport could have kept pace with Lord Wolseley's rapid advance; that any inconvenience that may have occurred was due to military exigencies and unforeseen complications with the Ottoman Government; and that, in the words of the communication to *The Times*, there were no failures of the working of the Supply and Transport Services at the seat of war, while from an administrative point of view the expedition was a success. In support of this view the one specific fact adduced is that the time which Lord Wolseley calculated as necessary for the occupation of Cairo was fifty-six days from the 21st July, 1882, and that that occupation was actually accomplished in fifty-five.

A DOUBLE-EDGED ARGUMENT.—It seems to me that this fact tells strongly in support of a very different conclusion. It shows at least that the end of the campaign was not appreciably accelerated before what was anticipated from the first. It incontestably proves that all arrangements made with a view to the campaign, which resulted in deliveries in Egypt after Cairo was occupied, must be regarded as utter failures. It shows that all arrangements carried out in such a manner as to be unavailable at Ismailia (the place from the beginning intended as the base of operations) in time to permit an army of 20,000 to land, fight at least one decisive battle, and reach Cairo on September 15th, must be regarded as having completely broken down.

The arrival of a landing pier barely a week before that date can scarcely be excused on the ground of military exigencies The conveyance at a cost of some £20,000 of a lot of mules, trained, equipped, and in possession of Government months before preparations commenced, from the Cape of Good Hope to Aden, five days from Ismailia, a week after the capture of Cairo, can hardly be called an administrative success. As to mules intended as reserve, we have nothing to do with them, but the fact that of 3600 of these animals intended for distribution of supplies from depôts, and costing, without freight or forage, over £90,000, not one-third were available for the purpose for which they were intended when Cairo fell, can scarcely be looked upon as successful administration. The fact that of 1650 muleteers and headmen intended to be hired in Malta, Cyprus, Italy, Turkey, and elsewhere, not 600 ever came to hand, and the fact that 500 at last ordered from India landed, or, if not countermanded, might have done so, after the war was over, does not to an outsider look very like a success. Nor does the fact that the Iron Ration intended for the campaign was first available at Cairo. The dispatch of seventy days' supply of unsuitable flour, and the way in which it was gone about, can hardly be said to have had anything to do with military exigencies, nor can the purchase of £20,000 worth of hay, worse than useless for the purposes of a campaign. As to unforeseen difficulties in Ottoman territories, where the Government imprisoned or threatened to imprison everyone who had anything to do with us, it hardly required a prophet to foresee them, and they were not unforeseen by the Commissary-General when he formally protested against our relying on Turkey at all. The world was open to us; our own Colonies and dependencies lay scattered over every portion of the globe, and what right had we deliberately to select Turkey, whose attitude on the Egyptian question the whole world knew, to lend ourselves to the corruption of her officials and to carry off her subjects in open violation of her laws? It may be said that the seizure of Ismailia was precipitated by circumstances, and occurred earlier than was originally contemplated. That is possible, and we have no direct evidence on the point, but it could not have been precipitated by many days, for every military and naval preparation had been made when the event occurred. The plea, however, has not been urged, and we may be tolerably certain that could it have been sustained it would not have been so long concealed.

"The Rapid Dash Forward."—The argument that the rapid dash forward disconcerted transport arrangements may be a good one in the case of transport which had arrived while the rapid dash forward was being made. That period however, closed when Kassassin was occupied on August 26th, and on that date the regimental transport was still incomplete, a mere fraction of the Departmental Transport, and none of the auxiliary, had arrived at Ismailia, or was in a position to outstrip. At that date, too, and for long after, the vessel to lift out the engines had not arrived, the locomotives purchased in England had not arrived, the rails sent out had hardly been got at, and the efficiency of the transport from the base, such as it was, was still further impaired by the fact that it was not placed under the orders of the General of the Line of Communication till a week after the occupation of Kassassin.

A Word for the Commissariat Department.—There is a word of explanation which, in justice to one department, ought not to be longer delayed. Many of the facts which I have narrated having already, in a fragmentary form, transpired in connection with an enquiry into the working of the Commissariat and Transport Services, a large portion of the public has not unnaturally jumped to the conclusion that the Commissariat and Transport Department of the Army was to blame for every shortcoming disclosed. How far that department may be censured or commended by the Select Committee I cannot of course say, but this I can say, that it had nothing, or next to nothing, to do with any of the occurrences detailed above. The Commissariat Department, for example, had nothing to do with the selection of flour, which was made contrary to the advice of its Chief. The much-abused hay was certainly purchased subject to inspection by a Commissariat officer, but it was little more than a nominal inspection, and was arranged for by another department without any consultation with the Office of the Commissary-General. The purchase of transport animals does not fall within the province of the Commissariat Department, and though the Commissary-General, having had considerable experience in the matter, tendered his advice, it was disregarded. He was indeed responsible for the *personnel* of his corps; but his request for labour was disregarded, and the moment it was decided to hire foreign drivers in the countries where the mules were to be purchased, though his responsibility continued his liberty of action was gone. His department had nothing to do with the selection of carts or shipment of stores, or in fact anything except estimating the establishment required for the campaign, which would doubtless have been sufficient had it arrived. The responsibility of the Commissary-General with the expedition did not commence till he landed in Egypt; and when, having received intimation of his appointment, he busied himself with suggestions and demands, he was given to understand that his interference was not desired. The uniform complaint of the officers of the Commissariat and Transport Department is—that under the existing system, in time of war they are debarred from performing the duties to which they are trained in time of peace, and are blamed for the miscarriage of supply and transport arrangements in carrying out which they have had no voice.

THE LESSON OF THE CAMPAIGN.—It appears to me that the result, which I have described, of so many costly arrangements, occurring as they did in a campaign where we were unopposed by sea, and feebly opposed on land, where the enemy left us a waterway which they might easily have drained, and a railway that they might at least have compelled us to re-lay—it appears to me that these results ought to teach us a lesson. If, disregarding that lesson, we should find ourselves brought into conflict with an enemy a little more nearly our match, and a little less apathetic or scrupulous* as to his means of defence, we should run no small risk of receiving another lesson such as it would be impossible to disregard. In Egypt it was simply a question of wasted treasure and minor privations. In Europe it would probably be a question of life or death. Little time is afforded in modern warfare to make up for the consequences of early blundering, and the destiny of more than one great nation has been settled within fifty-six days.

A NATIONAL QUESTION.—The efficiency of our military administration is a national and not a party question. If any one imagines that, had a different political party been in power, the Egyptian campaign would have been differently administered from home, let him read what is appended to this pamphlet regarding the Afghan war. That was conducted under a Conservative Cabinet, as the Egyptian under a Liberal one; and if the reader can find anything to be proud of in the Transport and Supply arrangements of either campaign as compared with the other, I envy him his powers of discrimination. Whatever Government is in power in nine cases out of ten becomes the passive administrator of whatever vicious system it may find in operation. Ministerial life is too short for the majority of Ministers to grapple with reforms, however much required, unless they are forced to do so by public opinion. That the facts set forth in the foregoing pages may have some effect in helping to frame public opinion is my hope. If not, they may at least prove interesting to John Bull as showing why his little wars are so costly and how his money goes.

---

* As an instance of the extreme scrupulousness of the Egyptian commander, Colonel Tulloch, Chief of the Intelligence Department, told the Committee that Arabi had made arrangements to cut the canal, "but there was a sheik who came down from "Upper Egypt and told Arabi that he had **no** business to cut the Sweetwater Canal, "as it was contrary to the principles of the Mahomedan religion to deprive human "beings of their food, and it was owing to that sheik that he **never** cut the canal."— Answer 5998.

APPENDIX.

HOW THE MONEY WENT IN THE AFGHAN WAR.

The following letter, which appeared in *The Times* of April 16th, 1882, explains itself :—

Sir,—At a moment when this country is about to pay India another half-million of her £5,000,000 contribution towards the expenses of the Afghan War, and when Ministers and ex-Ministers are wrangling as to the correct method of making the payment, it may possibly be of interest to the long-suffering British taxpayer to learn how his millions went.

Since I failed to secure an inquiry at the hands of a Select Committee of the House of Commons into the working of the Indian Commissariat and Transport service in the Afghan War, I have obtained copies of the "Administration Reports of the Indian Commissariat Department" for the official years 1878-9 and 1879-80. They were, of course, not meant to be made public, but as I am convinced that no reform will ever be obtained without full publicity, and as I am under no pledge of secrecy with respect to them, I beg to lay before your readers a few of the facts which they disclose, which will at least help to show how a large portion of the expense towards which this country is still contributing was incurred.

To indicate the importance of the department to which the reports refer, I shall commence by stating that the money drawn by it for departmental purposes during the two years in question amounted to no less a sum than 113,399,252 rupees, or say £11,000,000 sterling. The amount in inefficient balance or unadjusted in executive offices at the end of the official year 1879-80 was 10,325,939 rupees, or say £1,000,000. "This sum," says the Commissary-General (Colonel Willes), "will give some idea of the unavoidable state of the cash accounts of officers, though it gives none of the amount of work either done inefficiently or not done at all. . . . I trust it may be found when the time comes for closing the outstandings that nothing worse than delay and confusion have resulted from the excessive drain caused by the war on the department in all its branches, but that many an agent is making a fine harvest out of the war owing to the want of proper supervision is undeniable. . . . Once get a mass of arrears in any office and it becomes a paradise for dishonest clerks, who exist in every office, who have a horror of speedy adjustment of accounts, and whose sole object is to make frivolous and petty objections."

Now who was to blame for the state of things which the Commissary-General thus forcibly condemns? No person, of course—the system, as with ourselves, of divided responsibility and general cross-purposes. To understand this it is necessary to revert to the beginning of the war as set forth in these reports.

Shortly before Sir H. Norman left India Colonel Willes had called his attention to the utterly inefficient state of the Commissariat and Transport Department, and pointed out the inevitable consequences should war break out. Sir Henry's reply was, "Wait till war does break out, and then see how we will shell out the money ; you will have everything you want then." To which the Commissary-General answered, "It will then be too late." When the Afghan War broke out, according to the Commissary-General, his department was "on the most limited peace scale, quite insufficient even for that." In August, foreseeing the probability of hostilities, the Commander-in-Chief urged the Commissary-General to be communicated with, with a view of making preparations, but the Government refused its permission, and an invaluable opportunity was lost. Six weeks later Colonel Willes was told to prepare. The first step was to obtain from the army officers to supplement the department. On going to the Adjutant-General to arrange for this, that officer "expressed his surprise, and stated that the whole question of transport had been settled, and the officers for the duty detailed." He expressed more surprise when he learnt that the Commissary-General had never been consulted on the subject by the Quartermaster-General, who had drawn up the scheme. The Commissary-General thereupon appealed to the Military Member of Council, who had also heard nothing of the arrangement, and who summarily cancelled it.

This occurred at the end of September, 1878, on the very eve of the war. With such a commencement it was hardly likely that things would work smoothly. With General Biddulph's column some 6000 camels, which it was intended should go no further than Dadur, and thence return to Mithankote to form a train, were carried on to Quetta, "and kept there, though not required, against the remonstrance of the senior commissariat officer, Colonel Lane. At Quetta there was no food for the large number of camels, which simply starved and died in enormous numbers. . . . Had they been at once returned, vast numbers would have been saved," and been available for services for which they were urgently required. Again, an order reached the Commissary-General from the Quartermaster-General on the 18th of October, 1878, to the effect that General Stewart's column was to march on the 1st of November, "though at the time there was not a single animal available, and I (Colonel Willes) was never asked if the means of moving this force existed. Eventually the order was cancelled and the column was sent on by rail."

When the Treaty of Gandamak was signed, it may interest the British taxpayer to know that some £25,000 maunds of stores—a bazaar maund is 82lb.—were presented to the Ameer. "The whole of the carriage when it returned to India, whether camels, mules, or ponies, was completely exhausted, and very few, even after long rest, were again fit for any work. It was evident that the work, climate, want of supervision, and limited and unsuitable food had completely broken down the whole of the transport of the army." "It has been ascertained that during the whole of the past winter, when transport animals were being passed up from Peshawur to Jhelum, they seldom got their full allowance of food." They were, in fact, under charge of utterly unreliable men, "sometimes chuprassies at five rupees a month," who starved them and plundered the Government. The gear supplied for the mules and ponies proved "very unsuitable." "The state of the Peshawur cantonments, consequent on the enormous number of dead animals lying about, threatened a serious outbreak of sickness," and "the sick transport throughout the whole campaign was unsatisfactory." So much for the first phase of the war.

"As at the commencement of the first campaign," writes the Commissary-General, "so to the very end, there was the same strain on the department to provide the necessary carriage," which owing to the enormous demand and mortality and the necessity for sending back the sick and weakly animals from the Khyber, rendering it an almost hopeless task to provide the means of moving the troops and feeding them. . . . In reality, as regards the transport, the army was worse off at the commencement of the second, than the first campaign." The existing transport was "thoroughly used up," and it was necessary to go to distant provinces for fresh animals. The difficulties were overcome, but at enormous expense. A depôt was established at Jhelum at a cost of 45 lakhs of rupees—£450,000. There were many ponies from all parts sent up to Jhelum quite unsuited for transport work, and the expense thus incurred unnecessarily was very great. . . . In many instances it is impossible to imagine how the weedy, miserable creatures were selected." As usual, the pony gear was "found faulty in every respect," and the pack-saddle made up at great expense according to standard patterns was "generally altered at Jhelum to meet Captain Wintle's views." The Bombay Government having much spare carriage available in Scinde, "was good enough to place some of it at the disposal of the Bengal Commissariat." In the lot were 262 camels, which arrived at Jhelum in such miserable condition that 146 died, two were shot, 12 sold, and only 102 went to the front. "I saw a telegram to Sir M. Kennedy," writes Colonel Willes, "in reply to one of his, commenting on the unnecessary expense of sending such sickly animals, stating that they would have died if kept in Scinde. They had better have done so."

The carts, 586 in number, were of various builds. "The wheels were generally very bad, and when those deemed fit for use were passed to Peshawur they fell to pieces in great numbers on the road."

It had been decided to institute a cart train for Jhelum, and an offer was made by the acting Commissioner of Patna to supply 1500 carts with bullocks in a very short time at 150 rupees each. Although Commissary-General Willes objected that Patna carts were not suitable for the work required, and his opinion was fortified by the Lieutenant-Governor of Bengal and the Commissioner of Patna, the offer was accepted. "On arrival the carts were found to be totally unsuited for the work required of them. Indeed, they seemed to be absolutely rotten and worthless, and proving so useless caused the first delay in completing the military transport train, as carts and bullocks had to be purchased in the Punjab, and the arrangements commenced *de novo*." The camels were placed in charge of ignorant attendants, "and until these became accustomed to their work the state into which camels fell, from neglect and ignorance, was absolutely horrible, such sores as were found on the animals being noisome in the extreme." Again, we are told the attendants sent with the camels "were badly paid, and often not paid at all. They were only anxious to be freed from a disagreeable service, and consequently neglected the animals, hoping that when they died or became useless they would be free to return home." In my recent speech on the subject, which you were good enough to report, I gave from another and equally reliable source details of the atrocious mismanagement and cruelty to which the 90,000 camels and other baggage and slaughter animals, estimated to have died in the war, were subjected, and I need not dwell longer on this subject. There is, however, another matter to which attention should be called. In October, 1878, the Commissary-General suggested "that the Adjutant-General should submit, for the sanction of the Government, proposals for the audit of the accounts of commissariat field charges, and more especially as regards relaxation of the ordinary rules of audit." He desired, as he elsewhere explained, that field account offices should be established; that the rules as regards vouchers, easy to obtain in time of peace, but often impossible to procure in the field, should be relaxed; and that legitimate payments, concerning which there could be no doubt, should be looked into speedily, and accounts settled with as little delay as possible. He was backed up by Colonels Sibley and Brand, who based their arguments on the experience of past campaigns, in which, as Colonel Brand remarked, till the campaign was over no accounts were attempted, opening thus the door for various forms of false charges, false rates, fictitious purchases, short credits," &c. The Commissary-General's proposal, he tells us, "met with determined opposition from the Account and Military Department at Calcutta," and he only succeeded in getting it (or, rather, a portion of it) sanctioned by an appeal to the Viceroy in Council. Even then the accounts fell, as we have seen, much into arrear, "owing to the majority of the permanent clerks being withdrawn from the field, and the offices left in charge of officers totally ignorant of commissariat accounts, and the duty to all of whom was most disagreeable, because the pay was only 150 rupees and the responsibility excessive."

The officers employed generally objected, and in some cases earnestly protested against being put to the work, and apparently with good cause—for one of them, at the date of Colonel Willes's report, found that he could not retire, having 20 lakhs (£200,000) to his debit. Yet, when there was such an urgent demand for skilled clerks, says Colonel Willes, " I notice that a mass of statistics has been issued by the Examiner of Commissariat Accounts with his annual report for 1878-9, reviewing the cost of various articles, such as fowls, eggs, grain, at one station as compared with another, which must have required a large number of clerks to work out. When lakhs, if not crores, of rupees were being spent on account of the war, I would submit," he adds, "that the preparation of such statistics might well have ceased, and the clerks been sent to various account and executive offices, where their services, being experienced men, would have been invaluable, and have, in a great measure, prevented the arrears which accumulated." These arrears, as I have already stated, on Colonel Willes's authority, amounted to over 10,000,000 rupees, and afforded "a fine harvest for many an agent" and "dishonest clerk." As an example of the working at cross purposes which prevailed in this, as in other matters, I will only add that, according to the Commissary-General, "an attempt was apparently made, shortly after the establishment of the account offices of the first campaign, to represent that the plan had not worked satisfactorily ! " that he was ordered to furnish certain information to the Examiner of Commissariat Accounts at Umballa ; that he replied, furnishing the information requested, and suggested that the Accountant-General, Military Department, should inspect certain field account offices, with a view to placing matters on such a footing as would expedite the adjustment of accounts. To his report he had no reply, and, though the Government approved the Accountant-General making the inspection, "what his report may have been," says the Commissary-General, "I am not aware, but the result of his action was never communicated to me."

When I moved for a Committee to inquire into the working of the transport in the Afghan War I gave abundant evidence of the extent to which its breakdown impeded the movement of our troops, the horrible cruelty inflicted upon the transport animals, and the enormous waste of public money involved. I was told that the matter had been looked into, that its importance was recognized, and that there was no danger of any similar breakdown in future. Private information from a well-informed quarter leads me entirely to doubt this comfortable assurance, the more so as I find from Colonel Willes's reports that before the outbreak of the Afghan War he had in vain, and in many cases repeatedly, pressed for reform of a number of these defects in the system which our subsequent experience so disastrously revealed. Something has been done, of course, but nothing that can effectually remedy the deplorable state of matters disclosed in the report of Principal Veterinary Surgeon Collins, which lies in a pigeon-hole in the War Office, or the administration reports of Commissary-General Willes, from which I have given a few extracts above. It is all very well to vote so many millions of British money to assist India to bear the extravagant cost of the Afghan War, but I cannot help believing that we should be rendering her, and ourselves as well, a much more real and permanent service were we to insist upon a thorough investigation of the disgraceful state of matters which the long-concealed reports of Sir M. Kennedy, Mr. Collins, and Colonel Willes proved to to have existed, with a view to the radical reform of a "system" of commissariat and transport so extravagant, so unreliable, and so full of peril.

Yours most obediently,

CHARLES CAMERON, M.P. for Glasgow.

The following, extracted from "Hansard's Parliamentary Debates," is that portion of my speech in moving for the appointment of a Select Committee referred to in the foregoing letter to the "*Times*," which relates to the mismanagement of the Afghan War. I reprint it, as it deals with a part of the subject not touched on in the letter, viz.: the wholesale and atrocious cruelty to transport animals which disgraced that war.

He (Dr. Cameron) now came to the Afghan War. Telegraphing from Simla in June, 1879, *The Times* Correspondent said—

"It is earnestly to be hoped that the successful termination of the campaign may not prevent the fullest enquiry into the causes of mismanagement so discreditable and so dangerous. The Khyber Force was," he adds, "for some time so helpless, owing to the want of transport, that they could not have advanced to Cabul if Yakoob Khan had defied us."

In March of the same year, 1879, an officer of high rank in our Army, in a private letter which he held in his hand, wrote—

"There is no doubt about the fact, which will come out some day, that the Candahar Force under General Stewart could not get on farther than Candahar owing to the great mortality among the transport animals."

Mr. Charles Williams, an experienced war correspondent, in his notes on the first portion of the Afghan War, said that, in consequence of the impossibility of bringing up food for the Kurrum Column, the Native troops had to be put upon half rations—

"Seven hundred camels died in a week, and in less than a month it came about that this column could neither feed itself nor move back for food for want of transport. Nor was it much better," he added, "with General Biddulph's column . and it is a matter of fact that General Lacey's brigade was kept oscillating on the road between Candahar and Giriskh in this wise—when provisions reached it from Candahar it moved towards Giriskh, three or four marches. As they were consumed, and the camels died, the brigade fell back towards Candahar until it met another convoy, when it resumed its march. And this was repeated not merely once or twice."

In his work on the Afghan War, Mr. Duke had published a letter from General Roberts, in which that officer wrote—"In the Kurrum Pass our great difficulty was want of transport;" and if he were to quote from the work of Mr. Howard Hensman he might multiply evidence to the same effect. The history of the whole campaign was, however, summed up by a well-informed officer, who had written to him (Dr. Cameron) in this single sentence—"Over and over again our columns could not move for want of transport." Had they been in this condition in the presence of a daring and enterprising foe, the inability of the troops to move must certainly have led to disaster. He would not argue the question as to whether camels were the proper animals to employ in such a campaign; but, evidently, if used, only strong adult camels should have been relied upon for such service. But that was very far from being the system adopted by the Indian Department. Baby camels, camels incapacitated from age, ponies barely able to drag their own carcases through the campaign, were all bought up for the Transport Service.

"Anything more atrocious than the cruelty and neglect culminating in such tremendous losses as occurred in the Afghan Campaign I have never heard or read of."

These were the words of an officer of great experience, and thoroughly well entitled to speak on the subject.

"Putting aside," he continued, "the horrid cruelty, the direct loss must have been immense; but the indirect loss will be felt in the agricultural districts from which the animals were drawn for long years to come."

And in this connection Mr. Charles Williams mentioned that, in the opinion of the civil authorities in Scinde, one third of the available animals in Scinde were used up in the first phase of the Afghan War. And the officer from whom he was quoting went on to say—

"Veterinary science in the Afghan, as in the Egyptian Campaign, was utterly ignored by the Indian authorities. There was no veterinary organization—nothing but the grossest mismanagement as far as animals were concerned.

The Indian authorities entertained the utmost contempt for the dictates of veterinary science, and the result was that they neutralized in Afghanistan and afterwards in Egypt the elaborate precautions we took with the animals intended for the Transport Service of our troops. The letter from Simla already referred to contained the following words:—

"I forward by this mail *Civil and Military Gazette* of 19th March, 1879. It will give you an idea of the fearful mortality among the camels at the front, and really we cannot be surprised at the loss. I have been fighting for sanction for administrative veterinary officers to be posted with the various columns at the front; but the Government will not sanction the expense. However, acts are cropping up showing the grossest neglect—or, rather, I should call it rascality. Steele reports that out of 70 camels he examined lying dead at Quetta 26 were but two years old. Mr. Edwards, veterinary surgeon, reports that many of the female camels were with calf, and died of slipping their calves. Thousands of animals have died from neglect, ignorance, and rascality. The officers of the Transport have been chiefly taken from Infantry regiments, and are ignorant to a degree upon all subjects pertaining to animals. I have reported all this officially, and there is sure to be an investigation, and Government is sure to burke the whole thing."

From that extract it would appear that the facts had all been officially reported, and if the Committee were granted, he should be able to prove, by means of the Reports, the facts he had stated. The Report had, of course, been burked, as it was predicted it would be. He wanted the facts brought to light for the sake of the efficiency of the Service, because India was going on pursuing the even tenour of her way; and on the first occasion on which our troops had to co-operate with Indian troops, if let alone, she was sure to land us in some mess. He now came to the cruelty and waste. If the House thought the statements he had to make were incredible—and to his mind they were so horrible as to make him wish to be able to believe they were incredible—all he could say was that if he got the committee he undertook to prove every one of them. In the Kurrum column, of 6000 animals, 40 per cent. were reported as either too young, too old, or in other respects so physically incapable of performing the work of the campaign that it was sheer waste of public money to buy them. Everywhere the veterinary surgeons reported the same thing as to the large number of unfit animals purchased for the Transport Service in the Afghan campaign. Of a batch of 400 ponies inspected at Jhelum, 395 were condemned as utterly unfit for the work. Again and again he found it reported that when animals had been purchased under proper veterinary supervision, the fact that they had been so purchased was at once apparent, and among them the number of rejections for unfitness for work was not more than 5 per cent. But the Indian authorities treated veterinary opinions with the most profound contempt. They held, he was told, that the requirements of the veterinary surgeons were far too high, and maintained that what they wanted was baggage animals that could carry a load of so many pounds weight. Accordingly, they loaded the wretched animals, including the condemned ponies, and sent the 395 to the front with the rest. The result was that the miserable brutes died by the way, and we lost not only the money expended in purchasing them, but also the loads they carried. Anything more cruel than sending on animals unfit for such service was to him inconceivable. They stood as so many animals of burden on paper; but we lost both the animals and their loads.

No improvement in this state of things took place as the war went on, and it was estimated by competent authorities that in the two phases of the Afghan campaign no fewer than 60,000 animals and 30,000 other baggage and slaughter animals died; and of these it was estimated that at least one half died because they were utterly unfit for the work for which they were bought. He did not know the exact value of the animals thus purchased, but taking the camels at £20 a-head, the loss sustained in camels alone must have been upwards of £500,000 sterling, and the cost, directly and indirectly, to the British taxpayer in beasts and material, including the loss caused by the delays from the breakdown of the transport, must have amounted to many times that sum. And now he came to the cruelty, and he ventured to say that any man with the smallest feelings of humanity would shudder at the barest recital of it. From every quarter it was described as having been simply atrocious. The transport animals were in charge of ignorant native salootries or farriers. Infectious diseases were rife amongst the animals, and no precautions were taken to prevent their spread. Animals suffering from rinderpest, scabies, glanders, and pleuro-pneumonia were beaten forward with the rest without any precaution taken to separate them, and the consequence was that every elephant in the Kurrum column got the foot-and-mouth disease, and in some cases the soles of their feet sloughed off, carrying the nails with them. No provision was made for shoeing animals; and at a dozen stations visited by one veterinary officer there were no shoes, no nails, no workmen. No care was taken to prevent sore backs; there were no dressings, no medicines, no instruments. It was with difficulty veterinary surgeons could get sacking to put over wounds to keep off the flies. At Quetta, out of 15,000 animals, 80 per cent. of the ponies and 20 per cent. of the mules suffered from sore backs. At Cabul there were 1700 cases of sore backs. Hon. Members might think it absurd to make so much fuss about sore backs; but the sore backs to which he referred were such as, by their extent and fœtor, sickened even the most experienced veterinary surgeons—backs on which the packs had eaten through the muscles and laid bare the ribs beneath. Sore backs swarming with maggots, backs in camels in which the sores had laid bare the spinous processes of the vertebræ, and in which the tissues were so infiltrated with purulent matter that when, to put them out of pain, the wretched beasts were shot, the coverings of the back gave way with the shock of the animal's fall, ejecting the fœtid contents to a considerable distance. Such a state of things might seem incredible, but if he were granted the committee he asked for, he would be prepared to prove that what he had said was literally true. It might be said such cases were rare; they were not rare, they were common. From everywhere he had the same testimony. One gentleman going through the Bolan Pass counted as many as 300 dead camels on one side, and 200 on the other, and saw many others dying, and the ravens picking out their eyes while they were yet alive. He could multiply instances of this kind, but would content himself with one wholesale case. Between October and December, 1880, 2000 animals were sent to Sherawak to pick up. Of course there was no veterinary surgeon in attendance. In the month of March the animals that survived were sold by auction. They numbered but 10 or 15; all the rest were rotting in the valley. The same mismanagement existed from the beginning to the end of the Afghan War, and the same mismanagement was repeated in connection with the Egyptian War. Among the witnesses as to the cause of the Afghan breakdown was General Showers, who ascribed the failure in the transport arrangements as largely to the absence of all administrative veterinary control. He said—

"The fact of there having been no administrative veterinary officer with any of the columns will hardly be credited."

Since this report the Indian Government, so little economical in many other affairs, had been guilty of the economy of cutting down their veterinary staff one-third—from 70 to 46. When they sent their contingent to Egypt, there were only four veterinary surgeons attached to it. Two of these went on with the troops, and two only remained with the transport, which embraced 6000 or 7000 animals. In our British forces we considered it necessary to send one veterinary surgeon for every 250 or 300 animals. The result of this Indian arrangement was that glanders was introduced into Egypt once, and rinderpest on two separate occasions, despite elaborate precautions by our own Veterinary Department. He did not propose to offer any suggestions as to how this state of things should be remedied. He could, if necessary, quote a number of what appeared to be common-sense suggestions that had been made ; but it was his opinion that what was above all things required was a knowledge of the facts and of the extent of the evil. If the committee he asked for was appointed, it would have no difficulty in finding numbers of competent men to make suggestions ; and he would very much rather trust to the common sense of a committee of the House of Commons for a reform of the evils which he had endeavoured to expose, than trust the matter to the consideration of a departmental committee of experts.